Two Girls Want a Puppy

By Ryan and Evie Cordell   Pictures by Maple Lam

HARPER

An Imprint of HarperCollinsPublishers

For our kids, Cadence, Emerson, Rorik, Jonas, and Jude, and for our much-loved pups, Millie and Hero

—R.C. and E.C.

For Mom, Dad, and my sister, Denise —M.L.

Two Girls Want a Puppy
Text copyright © 2015 by Ryan and Evie Cordell
Illustrations © 2015 by Maple Lam

ISBN 978-0-06-229261-2

The artist used watercolor and colored pencils to create the illustrations for this book.
Typography by Dana Fritts
15 16 17 18 19   SCP   10 9 8 7 6 5 4 3 2 1
❖
First Edition

Hi! I'm Cadence and I really want a puppy.

And I'm Emi and I really, **really**, *really* **want a puppy!**

This is our dad. He's **skeptical**.

He doesn't think we should get a puppy.

But we're going to prove him wrong.

Because we have . . .
a BRILLIANT
PLAN!

Dad always tells us to be **persistent**.

That means we should never give up.

We're going to show him that we can be . . .

1. Super Persistent!

Can we get a puppy?

Can we get a puppy?

Can we get a puppy?

Can we get a puppy?
Can we get a puppy?
Can we get a puppy?
Can we get a puppy?

Dad also says we should be more **responsible**.
So we're going to show him that we can be . . .

2. Super Responsible!

We're going to take care of Buick, our neighbors'
dog, while they're away on vacation.

We feed him

and play ball.

We give him a bath.

We even clean up after him!

"Buick's a grown-up dog.
He already knows how to sit, and
stay, and come when he's called.
He's not as much work as a puppy.
Puppies have to be trained.
Sorry, kids," Dad says.
"You are not ready."

Okay, we are **persistent** and **responsible**. Now we will show Dad that we are . . .

3. Super smart!

We're going to research puppies and
learn as much as we can about them.

"Dalmatian puppies are born all white and develop their spots as they grow," Mrs. Hoff tells us.

"The most popular breeds for police dogs are German shepherds, Belgian Malinois, and Dutch shepherds," says Officer Jay.

Wow! Dogs dream when they sleep, just like people!

Cool! Dogs drink water by forming the backs of their tongues into mini cups.

Dad notices how hard we've been studying.
He seems impressed!

Dad likes when we do things in new and
interesting ways. Now we're going to show
him that we can be . . .

4. Super Creative!

We'll write our own book about dogs!

• People have lived with dogs for tens of thousands of years.

"I had no idea that there are about **eight million** dogs in shelters who need forever homes," Dad says.

"WOW!"

"You girls are
persistent,
responsible,
smart, *and*
creative.
I'm very proud of you!
I think we're ready to . . .

"adopt a PUPPY!"

Thank you!

Thank you!

Thank you!
Thank you!

Look at all of these cute dogs in the shelter!
How will we ever pick just one?

But *one* puppy stands out.

She's the **perfect dog** for our family.

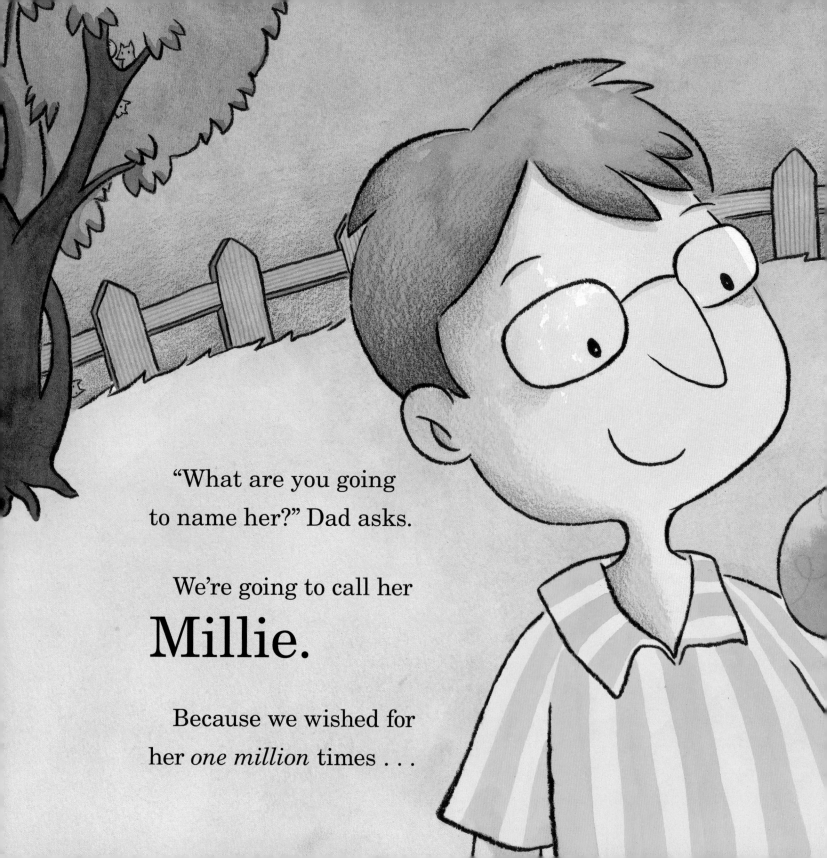

"What are you going to name her?" Dad asks.

We're going to call her

Millie.

Because we wished for her *one million* times . . .

and now she's ours!